MW00626042

REALLY

FUNNY

THING

ABOUT

APATHY

THE REALLY FUNNY THING ABOUT APATHY

Chelsea Martin

SUNNYOUTSIDE
Buffalo

ACKNOWLEDGMENTS

"McDonald's Is Impossible" originally appeared in *No Posit* and "Moments Before the Future Begins to Approach" originaly appeared in *Spork*.

Author photograph by William Schultz.
Used with permission.

ISBN: 978-1-934513-24-8

sunnyoutside
PO Box 911
Buffalo, NY 14207
USA

www.sunnyoutside.com

for
Z

Before it is possible to reach a goal, one must first arrive at every possible interval between the starting point and the goal. This is indeed an infinite number of tasks, given the infinitely divisible intervals.

AT THE END OF THIS STORY THE DOOR WILL OPEN AND UNDER EIGHT SECONDS WILL HAVE PASSED

I HEARD A KNOCK at the door and got up to answer it.

While walking toward the door I thought, "Who could it be?" and made a mental list of the possibilities.

My mom.

Aaron, Jim, Christina, Max, or Stephanie.

Dave.

My landlord.

A neighbor.

Someone who was lost.

Someone delivering flowers to me from a secret admirer.

A bad person.

A ghost.

Or a child selling something.

I thought that Dave, person delivering flowers, and ghost were the least likely.

And that neighbor and landlord were the most likely.

I wondered what the likelihood was that all of these people had come to my door simultaneously.

Mathematically, the chances were pretty high. Like one in a hundred, maybe.

Well, one in a hundred if each person's only possibilities were at my door or not at my door.

But psychologically, I think a person would hesitate going to a door that already had someone in front of it.

A socially apt, psychologically sound person would wait until the first person left before coming to the door.

Maybe I would have a succession of people knocking on my door today, each waiting for the person ahead of them to leave. What were the chances of that?

There had been a few instances in my life when one of my friends randomly showed up at my apartment when I already had someone over. It made me feel powerful. Necessary. Badass.

I would also feel this way if I received multiple phone calls from friends while I was already hanging out with someone.

When this would happen I would act extremely cool and unresponsive. I tried to emit the sense that this happened to me on a daily basis and I didn't care whom I talked to or whom I didn't talk to and that I just went through life surrounded by people and didn't have to try very hard.

Perhaps, I realized, this attitude was unbecoming.

I decided that whoever was at the door would receive an honest reaction from me regarding their presence.

If it was someone I was excited to see I would act excited.

If it was a neighbor I would act like I didn't care about the neighborhood watch program.

I wondered what my honest reaction would be if it was Dave at the door.

What were my honest feelings?

If he showed up here and was hurt or otherwise needed my immediate help, I would forgive everything immediately and do whatever I could.

If he came over to retrieve the sweater and wristwatch that he had left here, I would tell him that this perfectly illustrated our time together, that he was always thinking about himself and of course couldn't be bothered to consider what seeing him would do to me and to fuck off about the sweater and wristwatch.

If he were here to apologize to me, I would tear up and tell him that everything was my fault but that he should leave right away.

If he were here with another girl I would I don't know.

What were the chances, considering math and psychology, that Dave was here with another girl?

If Dave were here with another girl I would tell them that their visit was extremely improbable.

I would ask them if they felt like a very small number after a series of zeros behind a decimal point.

Maybe every action and event in the world was extremely unlikely, considering all the options.

It seemed clear to me that this was the case.

Maybe there were people who lived their lives under this notion.

People who woke up and thought, "Well, I guess I'll begin my random sequence of events now," and went to their window equally prepared to see their front yard in a normal state, or toilet papered, or burned down, or missing, or filled with people, or filled with marbles, or painted orange.

And they went to work in whatever clothes they had slept in.

And they borrowed money and returned it to someone else.

And they used Wite-Out to cover all the dates on their calendars.

And used spit balls or Band-Aids when they ran out of Wite-Out.

And they watched the same movies over and over, marveling at the predictability.

It seemed like everything would be disappointing if you had no expectations.

I had expectations.

I expected some sort of conversation to happen when I opened the door.

Unless I had been doorbell-ditched, which was another possibility.

Or someone had left something for me in front of my door.

It seemed like that had happened to me before but I knew it hadn't.

I had seen it happen so many times, to other people, in movies.

I had seen people fall in love in movies, too, and felt in love from it.

And I had seen people die in movies and it seemed more real than death in real life.

In real life you might be far away when death happens, and not have seen the person in several months or more.

Or years.

It happens.

And you might feel so detached that you don't even break your dinner plans after you hear.

And you can't seem to realize that your life has changed.

Because it hasn't.

Because you keep doing the same things you did before in the same order for the same reasons.

Months later, though, you'll have a partial memory of something, some old song you can't quite remember the lyrics to, and you'll think of calling them to clarify.

Because they definitely know.

Knew.

And that's the first time you realize that your life has been affected by this death, and it feels very surreal and meaningless and disappointing and you feel pathetic and selfish.

Death in movies is always very emotional and special.

Always moving.

Usually important or tied into the plot somehow.

I wanted to die in a movie.

I wanted to be well-lit and accompanied by soft piano music.

In a movie I had seen recently, there was a scene in which two people looked at each other and made subtle facial expressions back and forth that conveyed very little.

I belonged in that movie.

I felt that I understood the feeling portrayed in that scene at a higher level than I understood any other feeling.

Sometimes I heard my brain make sarcastic comments.

Comments like, *Oh, brother* and *Thank you.*

It happened when I was thinking about the scene from that movie.

I was thinking, "I understood the feeling portrayed in that scene at a higher level than I understood any other feeling," and I heard my brain say, Oh, that is so interesting.

My critical little brain.

It knew about all my insecurities. It knew about everything.

There were people in my life who seemed to have that same power over me.

Who seemed to be able to see inside me, view my motivations, immodesties, worries.

Saw things in me before even I was able to see them.

Dave wasn't one of these people.

It was easy to sneak certain words into conversation, lead him to thoughts that he would think were his own.

It was easy to make him feel what I wanted him to feel by telling him highly inaccurate personal stories about myself.

I rebuilt him and made him into a less secure, less interesting version of myself.

Everyone thought I was manipulative.

Because I told them I was.

And they found reasons to believe me.

People believed anything you told them as long as it was something unflattering about yourself.

And people liked you more if they could see them-selves in a slightly more flattering way through you.

It seemed possible to only see myself through other people.

It seemed impossible to look at my own Facebook profile without someone else's opinion in mind.

Or to send someone an MP3 without listening to it first,

pretending I was them, imagining that their interests and selectively told memories were mine.

Judging the lyrics as if for the first time.

Trying to gauge how they would affect their perception of me.

I wasted a lot of time over the years doing this.

It was hardly ever useful.

What if I had spent that time doing push-ups? Or polishing my shoes?

Or what else?

Looking out of windows or something, I don't know.

Or maybe it was useful.

Maybe I was actually channeling other people's reactions to things.

Maybe I had significant psychic connections with others.

It was possible.

Sometimes I received text messages from people about things right as I was about to send them a text message about the very same thing, on a day when there were no previous text messages between us.

Spooky.

Or I would be having a conversation with someone about San Francisco and the person would say something about a fear of rolling backward down the steep iconic hills and it would jog this childhood memory of throwing a tire down a windy hill and the tire following every impossibly sharp turn and rolling toward the highway, and I would remember very clearly the horrifying fear that the tire I threw would cause an accident, and running up the hill to hide in the brush and bushes and waiting and thinking that every semi-melodic noise was a police siren coming to get me.

And then the person I was having a conversation about San Francisco with would begin a story about an ambulance racing past him with its siren on while going up a steep iconic hill.

And I would think that the only only only plausible explanation that we both internally came to personal stories about sirens is that we had a psychic connection.

But I would never say anything.

Because I thought that if others didn't know about the psychic connections I had with them, that I could somehow use it as a tool for manipulation.

I was into innovative manipulation.

I laughed at people's dumb jokes using an obviously fake laugh so they would think I was uncomfortable not laughing at their jokes so that they would think I felt slightly-to-moderately inferior to them so they would attain a false confidence that I would convince them to use to flirt with the doorman so that we could get into places and meet the interesting people I wanted to meet.

Actually, I never did that.

If I ever told anyone about that, there would be no way to take it back.

People don't trust manipulators.

Even if the manipulation is well-intended.

I never hurt anyone in a conversation-worthy way.

I wanted things to happen, and I invented that want in others. It's not a big deal.

It's something you just do when you're smart enough to think of it.

I wanted to make people think I was manipulative so that when I appeared weak they would think I was just trying to get something.

But I was actually weak and didn't want anyone to know.

I half believed that the world made sense and I just didn't get it.

And that something would happen to me someday that was so exact and meaningful that it would make me realize why movies always seemed so contrived.

And I would start making movies.

Really great blockbusters.

*B*efore overtaking an object in motion, one must arrive at the object's starting point. During the time it takes to reach its starting point, the object will have advanced a certain, shorter distance. The pursuer must then advance to that new point, from which the object has undoubtedly already moved.

MOMENTS BEFORE
THE FUTURE BEGINS
TO APPROACH

ONE DAY I WOKE UP and my mom was hovering over me.

"You got a new email," she said. I asked her what she thought she was doing looking at my email.

"Oh, I wasn't. I set up a new account for you." It was an email from my dad, who I had never given serious thought to.

The Really Funny Thing About Apathy | 27

"Let's meet," the email said, and then went on to use various Internet acronyms and explain them inside of parentheses. We were to meet on December 10 at his brother's house. Coincidentally, his brother lived less than a mile away from us. December 10 was ten months away.

I snuck out of my house a lot at night during those ten months. Sometimes I'd lie on the golf course by myself, but mostly I'd meet up with friends and we'd toilet paper someone's house or ride our bikes to boys houses or sneak into homes that were being remodeled and steal boxes of new tile. One time we stole boxes of tile and laid it out on the driveway and sat on it for a little while and then left because we thought we might get caught. I can't remember going to school during this time.

I slept in a tent on a porch one time with two friends named Megan. The two Megans were going shopping the next day and I couldn't decide if I wanted to go or not. I sort of didn't want to go, but didn't know why. I woke up at 3 a.m. and my arm was burned and I didn't know why. Megan's mom was convinced it somehow had to do with aliens. I didn't know why she thought that. My mom thought it might have been caused by battery fluid that leaked from a flashlight onto my arm. I didn't remember using a flashlight. The whole night was a mystery to me.

Other weird stuff happened around this time.

I was in my bedroom at night with two of my closest cousins and we were sitting still listening to this sound we were hearing. A very rhythmic sound right outside my window.

"Like knives," Jaime said.

"Like a knife and a sharpener thing," Becca said.

I didn't say anything but I was excited that something was happening. Then Jaime started screaming uncontrollably and left the room and me and Becca left my room and Jaime said she saw a face in my window and none of us would go back into my room that night.

A few days later the three of us were having a campout in my backyard and we had set up this tent and everything but we were sort of running around the yard like idiots, and being loud. It was sort of late. A neighbor flashed flashlights at us and we thought he was mad so we quieted down. A few minutes later we heard cars pulling up to the front of my house. We immediately thought, "Oh, shit," because I lived in a gated community and we thought someone had told Security that we were being loud. Security had ruined my birthday party the year before and made all the boys go home, which was odd to me. So we started to head back to the tent to pretend we're asleep but we heard the security guards coming through the side yard toward us. We all ran into the house and watched through the windows as these people rummaged through our tent and pulled our blankets out and everything. Then my mom got up and looked out the front window and noticed that the trucks in front of our house belonged to a painting company and not Community Security.

After that everyone was sort of edgy.

One night when just Becca was over, we heard some rustling outside of my window and went to tell my mom. But apparently she had already heard because she was in the dining room with a bat and told us she was going outside. Becca and I watched from the door but we couldn't really see anything because it was so dark. My mom started yelling and hitting the side of the house and the ground with her bat and Becca screamed and ran around the living room for some unknown reason.

My mom came inside and said she saw some glowing red eyes. There was some uncertainty about why the thing with glowing red eyes hadn't attacked her.

"It must have been on a leash," Mom said.

Other stuff, too. Like one day we came home from the grocery store and our door was wide open and my mom was convinced our phone was bugged. Stuff like that.

Maybe it was summer; maybe that's why I wasn't in school.

When summer ended my mom got a long-term substituting job at the high school. She was teaching freshman science and I was in her sixth period class. She taught us how to dig holes big enough for tomato plants and how to take Polaroid pictures of each other. There was probably some reading, too. I don't know. Her class felt like summer.

I befriended a girl named Cerena, who wore similar pants as me.

"No other girls around here wear parachute pants," she said. She meant it in a good way. We talked on the phone after school. After I had driven home with my mom and told her which boys I had crushes on.

Cerena visited another country and said she was buying me things, so I drew her portrait. She came back and gave me a cheap handheld fan and I gave her the portrait. She said she liked it but it made her realize how fucked-up-looking her mouth was.

*

On December 10 my dad emailed me to say the he had to reschedule our meeting. I was relieved. We were to meet on May 4 instead. He sent me a link to a music video. I can't remember if I watched it or not. My mom and I drove to my uncle's house anyway.

"I made guacamole," he said, "And these are some pictures of my kids."

"Those are your cousins," my mom said. My uncle's house was big and empty. He had a dog. He had an ugly couch that looked new. The TV was small and really far from the couch.

"I put mayonnaise in the guacamole," he said.

On New Year's Eve, Cerena and I went to a party at a friend's house where there would be bands playing. I kissed two boys that night: Sam, who tasted like sour cream and onion chips dipped in ranch dip; and Nathan, who would be my boyfriend the next week.

I would go over to Nathan's house every weekend and he seemed to do everything he could to avoid hanging out with me. He'd take a shower as soon as I got there, then invite his friends over and beg them to drive him places. He'd be gone for hours while I watched televised sports games with his boring friends.

On Valentine's Day Nathan's best friend called me and invited me to the wedding of a friend of his. Nathan was at the wedding. We had sex that night and he dumped me afterwards, saying that he needed to focus on finding a job. I held him all night while we slept. Cerena told me she would kill him, or her boyfriend would kill him, or her brother would kill him, and I believed her so I said it wasn't a big deal.

A few weeks later Nathan brought a wrench to the high school and used it to threaten a boy I vaguely knew. I thought it was a pretty funny thing to do. He went to jail.

I drank a lot more after that. Cerena and I took an after-school ceramics class and we would drink whiskey beforehand and smush clay around and then drunk-drive home. I had a desire to be reckless but Cerena had too many problems. One day she showed me a cut on her hip, telling me she couldn't cut her wrists because then people would see it and be worried. I asked her why she felt like cutting herself.

"I'm pregnant," she said. "Well, I'm not really pregnant, but that's what I'm going to tell my boyfriend."

★

On May 4 we showed up at my uncle's house again, even though we knew my dad wouldn't be there. I forget how we knew. My uncle had made guacamole again and my mom talked about how she would decorate his house if it were hers. She said she would put an island in the kitchen but I thought it would have to be a very skinny island to fit in that very skinny kitchen. I didn't eat the guacamole because I was afraid it had mayonnaise in it, although I wasn't sure if the mayonnaise thing was a joke.

"He's coming for your birthday," my uncle said. My birthday was on July 16. I got bored so I walked home and instant-messaged my friends.

"What does your screen name mean?" I typed to one of them.

"It's an abbreviation of a slang exclamation," he typed back.

"Cool."

Sometimes this particular friend would add the word *beautiful* to the end of ordinary sentences. I wanted to believe he was calling me beautiful, but it was always a little ambiguous.

"I'm watching TV, beautiful."

At 11 p.m. I called my mom's cell phone and asked when she was coming home.

"We're still eating dinner," she said.

"Guacamole?"

"No, we made some, um, dinner," she said. It sounded like a joke but I wasn't sure. I instant-messaged my friend about what had happened on the phone.

"Your mom is hooking up with your uncle," he typed.

"I'm very hungry," I typed back.

"Uncledad," he typed.

"Haha."

*

On the morning of my birthday, my dad emailed and invited me to his house in Los Angeles for the weekend of August 9. He offered to buy my plane ticket. I accepted his invitation and then swiveled my chair over to the far wall and yelled to my algebra teacher, who lived alone in the studio apartment next door.

"You're a mean one, Mr. Roach," I yelled in song, and waited to see if I would hear him do something, then yelled, "I wouldn't touch you with a ten-and-a-half-foot pole!"

Two days later in summer-school algebra, Mr. Roach told his class that he had spent the weekend barbequing steaks on the back porch with his wife and three dogs.

Dogs? Wife? Porch? I thought.

*

"Do you think we can make it next weekend?" my dad said, through the phone that my mom was handing to me.

"Hi," I said.

"That way your cousins can come. Art's kids. Your uncle Art. That way him and your mom can spend time together. I have no problem with that whatsoever, and you shouldn't either. It's funny, sort of. It's really funny, actually."

Saturday he said, "I meant Wednesday."

My family went to the community pool and a popular boy from my high school befriended my six-year-old brother.

"Your brother's hella cool," the boy said, and I felt slightly more socially adequate.

On Wednesday, my dad bought us train tickets for Friday. I packed my Walkman in case I got bored on the train.

The train conductor said the train ride would take twelve hours.

Dad called, "Take cab to Chinatown."

"Be there in twenty minutes."

*B*efore any movement is possible, one must perform the task that comes directly prior to that movement. And that task, too, will require a prior movement before it can be performed.

MCDONALD'S IS IMPOSSIBLE

EATING FOOD from McDonald's is mathematically impossible.

Because before you can eat it, you have to order it.

And before you can order it, you have to decide what you want.

And before you can decide what you want, you have to read the menu.

And before you can read the menu, you have to be in front of the menu.

And before you can be in front of the menu, you have to wait in line.

And before you can wait in line, you have to drive to the restaurant.

And before you can drive to the restaurant, you have to get in your car.

And before you can get in your car, you have to put clothes on.

And before you can put clothes on, you have to get out of bed.

And before you can get out of bed, you have to stop being so depressed.

And before you can stop being so depressed, you have to understand what depression is.

And before you can understand what depression is, you have to think clearly.

And before you can think clearly, you have to turn off the TV.

And before you can turn off the TV, you have to free your hands.

And before you can free your hands, you have to stop masturbating.

And before you can stop masturbating, you have to get off.

And before you can get off, you have to imagine someone you really like with his pants off, encouraging you to explore his enlarged genitalia.

And before you can imagine someone you really like with his pants off encouraging you to explore his enlarged genitalia, you have to imagine that person stroking your neck.

And before you can imagine that person stroking your neck, you have to imagine that person walking up to you looking determined.

And before you can imagine that person walking up

to you looking determined, you have to choose who that person is.

And before you can choose who that person is, you have to like someone.

And before you can like someone, you have to interact with someone.

And before you can interact with someone, you have to introduce yourself.

And before you can introduce yourself, you have to be in a social situation.

And before you can be in a social situation, you have to be invited to something somehow.

And before you can be invited to something somehow, you have to receive a telephone call from a friend.

And before you can receive a telephone call from a friend, you have to make a reputation for yourself as being sort of fun.

And before you can make a reputation for yourself as being sort of fun, you have to be noticeably fun on several different occasions.

And before you can be noticeably fun on several different occasions, you have to be fun once in the presence of two or more people.

And before you can be fun once in the presence of two or more people, you have to be drunk.

And before you can be drunk, you have to buy alcohol.

And before you can buy alcohol, you have to want your psychological state to be altered.

And before you can want your psychological state to be altered, you have to recognize that your current psychological state is unsatisfactory.

And before you can recognize that your current psychological state is unsatisfactory, you have to grow tired of your lifestyle.

And before you can grow tired of your lifestyle, you have to repeat the same patterns over and over endlessly.

And before you can repeat the same patterns over and over endlessly, you have to lose a lot of your creativity.

And before you can lose a lot of your creativity, you have to stop reading books.

And before you can stop reading books, you have to think that you would benefit from reading less frequently.

And before you can think that you would benefit from reading less frequently, you have to be discouraged by the written word.

And before you can be discouraged by the written word, you have to read something that reinforces your insecurities.

And before you can read something that reinforces your insecurities, you have to have insecurities.

And before you can have insecurities, you have to be awake for part of the day.

And before you can be awake for part of the day, you have to feel motivation to wake up.

And before you can feel motivation to wake up, you have to dream of perfectly synchronized conversations with people you desire to talk to.

And before you can dream of perfectly synchronized conversations with people you desire to talk to, you have to have a general idea of what a perfectly synchronized conversation is.

And before you can have a general idea of what a perfectly synchronized conversation is, you have to watch a lot of movies in which people successfully talk to each other.

And before you can watch a lot of movies in which people successfully talk to each other, you have to have an interest in other people.

And before you can have an interest in other people, you have to have some way of benefiting from other people.

And before you can have some way of benefiting from other people, you have to have goals.

And before you can have goals, you have to want power.

And before you can want power, you have to feel greed.

And before you can feel greed, you have to feel more deserving than others.

And before you can feel more deserving than others, you have to feel a general disgust with the human population.

And before you can feel a general disgust with the human population, you have to be emotionally wounded.

And before you can be emotionally wounded, you have to be treated badly by someone you think you care about while in a naïve, vulnerable state.

And before you can be treated badly by someone you think you care about while in a naïve, vulnerable state, you have to feel inferior to that person.

And before you can feel inferior to that person, you have to watch him laughing and walking toward his drum kit with his shirt off and the sun all over him.

And before you can watch him laughing and walking toward his drum kit with his shirt off and the sun all over him, you have to go to one of his outdoor shows.

And before you can go to one of his outdoor shows, you have to pretend to know something about music.

And before you can pretend to know something about music, you have to feel embarrassed about your real interests.

And before you can feel embarrassed about your real interests, you have to realize that your interests are different from other people's interests.

And before you can realize that your interests are different from other people's interests, you have to be regularly misunderstood.

And before you can be regularly misunderstood, you have to be almost completely socially debilitated.

And before you can be almost completely socially debilitated, you have to be abandoned by your entire group of friends.

And before you can be abandoned by your entire group of friends, you have to be suffocatingly loyal to your friends.

And before you can be suffocatingly loyal to your friends, you have to be afraid of loss.

And before you can be afraid of loss, you have to lose something of value.

And before you can lose something of value, you have to realize that even things you think won't change will change.

And before you can realize that things you think won't change will change, you have to have the same conversation with your grandmother forty or fifty times.

And before you can have the same conversation with your grandmother forty or fifty times, you have to have a desire to talk to her and/or form a meaningful relationship with her.

And before you can have a desire to talk to her and/or form a meaningful relationship with her, you have to love her.

And before you can love her, you have to notice the great tolerance she has for you.

And before you can notice the great tolerance she has for you, you have to break one of her favorite china teacups that her mother gave her and forget to apologize.

And before you can break one of her favorite china teacups that her mother gave her and forget to apologize, you have to insist on using the teacups for your imaginary tea party.

And before you can insist on using the teacups for your imaginary tea party, you have to cultivate your imagination.

And before you can cultivate your imagination, you have to spend a lot of time alone.

And before you can spend a lot of time alone, you have to find ways to sneak away from your siblings.

And before you can find ways to sneak away from your siblings, you have to have siblings.

And before you can have siblings, you have to underwhelm your parents.

And before you can underwhelm your parents, you have to be quiet, polite, and unnoticeable.

And before you can be quiet, polite, and unnoticeable, you have to understand that it is possible to disappoint your parents.

And before you can understand that it is possible to disappoint your parents, you have to be harshly reprimanded by one of your parents.

And before you can be harshly reprimanded by one of your parents, you have to sing loudly at an inappropriate moment.

And before you can sing loudly at an inappropriate moment, you have to be happy.

And before you can be happy, you have to be able to recognize happiness.

And before you can recognize happiness, you have to know distress.

And before you can know distress, you have to be watched by an insufficient babysitter for at least one week.

And before you can be watched by an insufficient babysitter for at least one week, you have to vomit on the other, more patient babysitter.

And before you can vomit on the other, more patient babysitter, you have to be sick.

And before you can be sick, you have to eat something you're allergic to.

And before you can eat something you're allergic to, you have to have allergies.

And before you can have allergies, you have to be born.

And before you can be born, you have to be conceived.

And before you can be conceived, your parents have to copulate.

And before your parents can copulate, they have to be attracted to one another.

And before they can be attracted to one another, they have to have common interests.

And before they can have common interests, they have to talk to each other.

And before they can talk to each other, they have to meet.

And before they can meet, they have to have in-school suspension on the same day.

And before they can have in-school suspension on the same day, they have to get caught sneaking off campus separately.

And before they can get caught sneaking off campus separately, they have to have somewhere to go.

And before they can have somewhere to go, they have to be familiar with McDonald's.

And before they can be familiar with McDonald's, they have to eat food from McDonald's.

And eating food from McDonald's is mathematically impossible.

*M*ovement of an object is broken up into fragments of time, like frames of a movie. There is no fragment in which movement actually occurs, because fragments are made from the smallest possible instants. In any given instant, the object is at rest, and so can never really move.

THE CONSUMPTION

I AM AT MY DESK in my own apartment, consumed, of course, with thoughts of Reid. How could he leave me? As my roommate, Netta, walks in, I quickly calculate the exact temperament and sociability level I should have at this hour, of this day of the week, given the variables of recent history that might influence these levels. I strike my pose of dreamy thoughtlessness as well as a weary eagerness for any breaking gossip about our mutual friends.

"Aaron and Naema are obviously dating," Netta says. "I don't see why they don't just admit it." I calculate a good reaction to this: a twice-removed frustration, a self-righteous shake of the head, and a meaningless comment such as, "What are we going to do with them." I add a sigh of acceptance. Netta flops on my bed and embraces my decorative pillow. I determine that this is the moment she expects me to ask about her romantic life.

"Jim wants to see me again, of course," Netta says. I calculate the right reaction to this, a poking inquisitiveness with slight but lighthearted jealousy. I ask her if they had talked recently and, if so, about what, and how she felt about him. I wonder if the position of my body is expressing that I want to have this conversation. I face myself toward Netta, my limbs becoming nothing but directional implements for the composition of this scene in my room, Netta being the focal point. I prod her faux-torturously for a few minutes about Jim, then cautiously, inconspicuously, become increasingly weary and distant until Netta grows bored and leaves my room.

*

I am standing alone in the kitchen with no real purpose, consumed, of course, with thoughts of Reid. Did he believe I would be strong enough to get through this without him? Nothing moves anywhere that I can sense. I am stagnating. I am moving through time, but each second, each snapshot of each second, is exactly the same. I think of Reid. I think of myself thinking of Reid. I think of myself holding Reid in a completely different snapshot in another point in time. I think of myself being the only one possessing this snapshot. I think of Reid possessing different snapshots, ones in which I am complaining about his breath or the movie he picked up for us. I think of myself breaking into Reid's apartment and swapping his snapshots for mine. Of waking up with all the unsatisfying snapshots that he must be holding onto and getting a sense of motivation or acceptance from this. Something moves in the refrigerator's motor and it begins to make an intrusive hum.

*

I am driving home from work in my car, consumed, of course, with thoughts of Reid. What was he doing at this very minute? In my rearview mirror, I see someone waving emphatically at me. They switch lanes and drive alongside my car and continue waving. I recognize him; he is a secondary or tertiary friend of Netta's, who has been over to our apartment several times for parties. I quickly calculate a response that would appease this guy, whose name I've forgotten, in an unmemorable way so he won't be encouraged to befriend me. I smile cordially as if he were a grocery store clerk or one of my grandparents' friends, and wave impersonally as I turn off on an exit that lengthens my trip home by seven minutes.

*

I am in the fetal position on my bed, consumed, of course, with thoughts of Reid. Had his toenails been clipped since the last time I trimmed them? The overhead light in my room flickers, and dies. It is my cue to begin sobbing, to draw connections from faulty wiring to my pathetic emotional state, but I don't have the energy.

*

I am at a garage sale that I have forced myself to go to because it's Saturday and I'm sick of cable and the garage sale is in my neighborhood anyway, and I am consumed, of course, with thoughts of Reid. Why had we never been to a garage sale together? A woman comes up to me and justifies the value of all the items around me.

"That toaster was only used once," she says, "at a wedding."

"That handkerchief was given to my daughter by the mayor himself."

"All of those records are very rare."

"The man on the cover of that magazine is Andy Dick."

"This tank top matches your shorts."

"My daughter bought this in Fresno."

"That cardamom is from a spice rack I was given on my birthday but I hate cardamom."

"Don't you love sudoku?"

I can't think of anything to say. I can tell she's trying to gauge what I'm looking at by the direction of my eyes, and I don't want any more explanation, so I look into the sky.

"It's a perfect day for a garage sale," she says. "I'm Helen."

"Hello," I say, pay her for the sudoku book, and walk the long way back to my house so she doesn't see that I live across the street.

*

I am alone in my bedroom, consumed, of course, with thoughts of Reid. Maybe someday I would find someone sort of almost close to as good. I receive a text message from my mother and realize that it has been over three weeks since we've spoken. I estimate her level of worry and decide to call her now, to get it out of the way.

"Oh, I just sent you a text," she says, "How is everything going?" I consider everything I know about my mother and determine that a specific reason for being too busy to call will most easily appease her. I determine the cause for my distractedness has to be something that will make her slightly uncomfortable and cause her to steer our conversation away from my life. A lie.

"I've been seeing someone," I say, and adjust my inflection to convey a hesitant excitability, an unstoppable momentum of sexuality and newness, flimsily restrained by our formal mother-daughter relationship. She lets it go.

"Well, your father finally fixed that sqeaky screen door," she says and I give a knowing snort of exasperated affection for my dad that invites her to describe the probably-long fight they had beforehand.

*

I am at work in my cubicle, consumed, of course, with thoughts of Reid. I'm thinking of a night we spent at my apartment when we mostly didn't talk to each other but not because we were upset, we were just comfortable. But maybe I had misinterpreted something. My boss pokes her head in. I calculate what kind of reaction my boss would want to see in an entry-level employee of five years, and tell her good morning with a composed, admiring enthusiasm.

"Are you able to work okay with this noise?" she asks. I have no idea what noise she is talking about. The whole world, to me, lately, has been a never-ending stream of unwanted noises. I hesitate to ask her which noise, specifically, she is talking about, as it might make me seem abnormal. *The* noise, she would say suspiciously, *the very apparent noise that everyone hears and is hindered by except, it would seem,* you. I quickly generate a broad response that will convey my commitment to hard work, as well as my pleasant normalcy, keeping the tone casual but hardworking.

"Oh yeah, you know, I just get into this intense focus mode and nothing bothers me," I say.

"Well in any case the repairman is coming sometime today, so you don't have to endure it much longer." I assume I'm not required to respond to this dead-end comment about a repairman, but she stands there patiently. I tried to produce a new topic of conversation that flowed seamlessly away from the repairman repairing something, since any further discussion would expose my ignorance to the 'noise.' A safe topic that would, ideally, lead to an end to this conversation.

"Well the weather is good, anyway," I say. I quickly identify this as a flawed remark; flawed because it could be the starting-off point of the eventual exposition of the part of me that isn't able to participate in conversations that are meaningless but still cohesive, the kind of conversations employees have with their employers every day. It was too disjointed from our previous statements about the repairman. But it was that last adverb, *anyway*, that pointed to my attempts to join two topics that had nothing to do with each other. But my boss agrees and adds some unmemorable statement about the ambiance of the office and taps my desk with her knuckles before she leaves.

*

I am walking from the offices toward my car, consumed, of course, with thoughts of Reid. Was he happier without me? As I get closer to my car, I notice a few flowers tucked into my windshield wiper. They are wild—I see the same flowers growing less beautifully a few yards away—but it is obviously intentional. It is the second time in two weeks I have found flowers like this in my car windshield. Part of me wanted to believe it was Reid who placed them there the first time, but now I can practically smell him, see his holographic body prancing over here with the flowers, then trying to find the most delicate, meaningful placement for them, communicating to me everything he was sorry for, letting me know he was wrong about everything. I imagine catching him in the act of tucking flowers into the handle of the door to my apartment. It is late at night and I hear the door handle moving, and so I go see who it is. My eyes tear up as I imagine myself repeating lines from the last scene of *You've Got Mail*, my lips quivering as adorably as Meg Ryan's as I say, *I wanted it to be you. I wanted it to be you so badly.*

I suddenly realize, helplessly, that this is a fantasy, and that the flowers have most likely been placed in my windshield by one of my homosexual male friends innocently flirting, trying to rack up points with me to solidify our friendship. Don't they realize how much this crushes me? I prepare myself for the disappointment. In the next few days I will be told who has done this and be expected to appear delighted by this information. I will have to find ways to convey that my loyalty to this person has increased tenfold, despite the fact any respect I had for them at all will crumble, and I will resent them immensely. They cannot be expected to understand that their innocent game has led me to rationally entertain thoughts I had been suppressing for months, effectually re-breaking my swollen, gasping heart. I will not make them pay in any perceptible way. It is possible, I am sure, to maintain the appearance of loyal friendship.

*

I am half asleep or mostly asleep on my bedroom floor, consumed, of course, with thoughts of Reid. His face is flashing through my head like a strobe. It seems like I can't remember anything but his face and the words I used to describe his face. No, I can't even remember the words to describe his face. There's nothing happening outside of my brain. I try to stay awake. Reid's face doesn't look like his face, and tomorrow will be no different from today. Sleep is a brief interruption and Reid's face is a stupid something.

It's a very long way to the bathroom from where I am.

ABOUT THE AUTHOR

Chelsea Martin currently lives in Oakland, California, and is the author of *Everything Was Fine Until Whatever* (Future Tense Books, 2009). Her website is www.jerkethics.com.